Games of our lives

A true story of Mandy Kloepfer with suggestions
on living life to the fullest now.'

You have the perfect body.

You are the perfect weight and height for your gender.

You have lots of friends and family members.

You get perfect A's.

You excel at everything you do.

You don't get in trouble.

STOP!

Do you really think that you are all that?

Do you really think that everyone is perfect?

Think again. No one is perfect according to what society thinks we should be.

We all come from a mixture of ethnicities and cultures.

We are all raised differently.

We were raised around different traditions and religions.

Some of us have parents of the same sex. And of course there is nothing wrong with this.

There is no manual that says how to raise a perfect child. There is no "for dummies book". The way we are raised up depend on all of the above factures.

How does society define us and how we are meant to be? Are we living that way or do we need to change?

Our differences are what makes us unique. Life is all about overcoming these differences to make it in this world. To make it is to live and be ourselves. We make our own decisions about how we act, how we eat, and how we dress.

Can we rightfully live if we all follow the same course of life?

Even with an injury that affects this we still have some input in these decisions. We do what we like to do and form relationships with the right people which will include family. The activities that we participate in is what makes each of us different from your neighbor, your family, your friends.

Of course there will always be someone who will tell you otherwise and that you can't.

In most instances you may get the urge to try and so what if you did fail. You now know that you can't but if you did, then you just proved the negative people wrong.

Are you listening to your peers or are you taking chances?

What would it be like to live in a world where each of us did the same thing? Not only would it be boring but this world that we live in would never advance. New perspectives would be minimal with all of us having the same background. Technology would not have advanced. We wouldn't be masters of technology teaching our parents.

Don't you just love children teaching parents on this technology?

There is a reason why migration happened hundred of years ago. This allowed us to learn from others and to build this world that we live in; we could adopt different practices, study different topics, and have different beliefs.

We learn to say no to things that are wrong or something that we simply don't like. Or at least we should, if not at first.

We learn from our mistakes only to be better at it the next time around. This allows us to grow which in turn pushes the world to grow.

From what I could remember I had a happy childhood. It was a joyful time of years spent at family Christmas parties and being in Girl Scouts. I made mistakes of course but I learned from them. I tried to not make the same mistake twice and that was always a great time.

Have you ever heard the song about friends in your life whether for a season or a reason? Friends will be an integral part of life and quite often you may not fully understand why they are there or why they have lost connection with you through life.

An unexpected event may be just the reason that they are pushed away.

In my case it was an automobile accident where I was tboned by a school bus. When I first arrived at the hospital I was in a coma with a severed spleen and my stomach was up in my chest. I was diagnosed with a severe TBI and brain stem damage. Doctors told my parents to put me in a nursing home and get on with their life. But they didn't listen. Those next few months were probably the most uncertain. No one could tell what I would do next if anything. And because I was on a 3rd shift schedule any of my purposeful movements happened in the evening or over night, many times of which were closed to visitors.

Maybe they are scared of you now.

Maybe they just don't know how to act.

Or maybe they just feel that likes and dislikes in activities will be different.

I had dysarthria which made my speech difficult to understand. This can get very frustrating when you have to repeat yourself several times.

And since it was hard to understand I was often treated that I needed everything repeated to me slowly and in the simplest language possible. Talk about frustration!

Perhaps there are now physical and/or mental barriers in your life and they don't how to react.

I was in a wheelchair when I left RIC. I moved to a walker right before I started therapy in Wheeling, IL. At wheeling RIC I progressed into a quad walker.

I didn't get to a single pole cane until I started PT in Belvidere, IL. Over time I'd work on walking unaided. And I still rely on the cane when I am walking outside. It can be frustrated because you can't walk fast and keep up with your peers.

Let's talk about running, that alone is nearly impossible with a cane! I hated running before and this just added to the frustration. I just wanted to feel free, wouldn't you?

I have had a couple of best friends. The first was Hannah who I met in school. We lived close so it was rather easy to get together and have fun together. I remember riding my bike down Sandy Hollow Rd to get to her house. We did sleepovers, hanging out with Myles, and even skinny dipping in her pool. That was awesome! We were also in Girl Scouts together.

We went separate ways in middle school exploring our own talents and thoughts. We had our own niche of friends now and we were not always on the same social level. We stayed friends, but the reason isn't clear why we no longer spent much time together.

Then I met Sarah in middle school and we stayed friends through high school and even graduation. We spent a lot of time together. Got in trouble together and make BK (Burger King) runs before school begin.

Sarah and I were both in the JROTC program as well as on the drill team. After my accident it seemed like she was scared, like so many. We no longer spent time together.

After Sarah came Kelly. Kelly came into my life after my accident. She didn't know me before and couldn't uphold me to what I was before. We enjoyed Dunkin' runs and just getting out of the house. Sadly she passed and once again I felt alone.

I've had many others come into my life and disappear just like that. The reason may not be clear as to why but we may one day understand why. Who really know when that will be?

Life is like a game of Uno. Sometimes we are dealt with cards that we can use right away and sometimes we are dealt with cards that we can't use. Instead we must wait to use them, strategically playing those cards that we can use until we can use those cards that we held onto. This is our life and achieving our own unique dreams.

What is your dream?

Every card that is played up until then results in the acclimation point in life at this end.

But is this really the end? We strive for this and will do what we can to achieve this point. Well at least that is what we are supposed to.

A point where you see no more moving forward until you encounter another event that causes you to move forward. Sometimes this is not even clear as you move towards it. This can be random. And it quite often is.

For me I can identify several acclimation points in my life.

The first was my dad passing when I was 14. That was very hard to deal with but it was something that I could overcome. This allowed me to be stronger in my mind and to help others through this difficult time.

What's great is that months earlier I was accepted into a Girl Scouts Wider Opportunity, Canoeing the Boundary waters. This just happened to be a few weeks after he passed. It was very difficult leaving but I had a great time and it was nice to get away from home.

At first I needed to accept it but the amount of time needed varies with each individual. Part of the length of time needed depends on how you were raised and what cards that you played in the game of life.

The next was when my mom remarried a wonderful man. That man, Ray, was also a widow. He had been through what my mom was going through and could helped her through it. Not to mention they were born on the same exact day with him only being a year older.

This taught me to be open and accepting. He brought with him a different set of values and cultural norms. This only allowed us to grow even stronger together.

The most current was when I was involved in a car accident. This taught me patience and taught me skills that I may have never unearthed. I have surpassed pretty much everything that doctors said that I wouldn't be able to do. And I continue to do it to this day.

Nothing is impossible, the word itself says I'm possible.

What are some of your acclimation points? How have they helped you in your life journey?

Or you could say that life is like a box of chocolates.

Some of the flavor you may like, and you eat those right away. Such as maybe the milk chocolate or dark chocolate.

Others are less desirable so you leave those in hopes that someone else may come along and eat them. If not, you end up eating them because they are left and you don't want to put them to waste.

Or would you rather be a scrooge and waste them? What is your choice?

What if those chocolates were like all the events in your life?

The desirable ones are all those events where you do what society wants you to do. You eat those chocolates like you follow societies path:

You are a perfect child doing nothing wrong.

You go to school and get Straight A's.

You get married and have a family.

You get to enjoy life without any struggle.

Then you are left with the undesirable chocolates where:

You grow old;

You gain weight;

You are struck with some kind of illness;

You fall and succumb to the circle of life.

So, if life were really like a box of chocolates where you have all the desirable chocolates first, think again!

Can you really choose exactly where you want to be years from now?

Well hypothetically you can but there is nothing saying that you will end up there.

Life IS NOT like a box of chocolates. You don't get to have all the desirable chocolates first -before the undesirable chocolates.

Instead think of life as a game of Uno. Some cards can be played right away while others must wait. You can have a master plan for all the cards in your hand but then the other player messes with it to get rid of the cards in their hands to be declared the winner.

As the game goes on you are dealt with other cards that might go against your plan but you are stuck with them because it is a game.

It is a game of life and although there is a board game with that name, it is not 100% accurate. Sure, you can choose from various careers, how many children that you want, and how much money that you will make.

But is that really accurate?

Can you really decide how many children you will have, how much you will make, and what you will end up doing for the rest of your life?

What about all the events in your life that you can't control?

What about those undesirable chocolates that you accidentally take a bite out of?

What about those cards that you are dealt that go against your master plan?

Are you able to overcome these differences that make you unique?

I had a great childhood, doing what I liked, had caring parents and siblings, had relatives that were there, and had friends that I liked to be around, I took part in clubs such as girl scouts and I knew how to say no.

So, like a box of chocolates where I got to have all those desirable chocolates or even a game of Uno where all these cards played by me and my opponent were in line with my master plan.

But then I got dealt with an undesirable card or ate a piece of chocolate that was not in my liking. My father passed away when I was 14.

Suddenly my plan for the cards in my hand changed. I needed to reorganize them all to stay in the game of life. I had to eat an undesirable piece of chocolate because no one else would play a card in my favor.

Those cards led me to a group of people that were not following the plan of life. They were in JROTC and so hanging around them made me feel popular.

How do we define popular?

Right then the cards in my hands were following a path. I could win with this plan.

But then the other player put a card down that threw off my plan. Just as it was before I had to reorganize in order to win.

My master plan somewhat changed. I was now dealing with the loss of my father. Eventually my mom did remarry and my step-dad filled that void in myself.

My master plan was back on track. Or was it?

Then it came down to the point where I had to decide what I wanted to do.

I could go to college where all the wise people went. Or I could follow the popular crowd and join the military. And of course, that is what I did.

I perceived them to be popular and to a point they were. Joining the military was full of activities that seemed interesting; following orders, knowing what to do and when to do them, firing off weapons in aims to hit that perfect shot.

My boyfriend at the time joined the Navy and I had this crazy idea to join the Navy. I did this behind my parents backs and boy were they surprised when I finally told them.

I ended up switching to the Army National Guard because I didn't want to leave home for 6 + years. What I learned in the military has helped me immensely in the life I have today.

But even in the military there were undesirable cards. You were always active and you had to meet a fitness standard. I had some difficulty reaching and maintaining this standard but I did it and boy was that awesome. Can you believe that I was 162 pounds standing at 5 feet 2 inches?

Again, it was the game of life.

We were not allowed to be unique.

We had to meet that standard in order to be kept.

We wore the same types of uniforms and couldn't add to it to make us unique.

These were events that needed to be followed.

Being a recruit led to a strict set of rules such as no candy, cell phones, or civilian clothing in the barracks.

Those events were like the undesirable chocolates or even the Uno cards that threw off your plan. You do them so you can get to a desirable piece of chocolate or even to get back to your master plan in Uno.

But what if being popular was more than that?

What if it didn't follow the game of life?

What if it did follow the game of life?

Coming back from the military was like coming back to the game of Uno where all the cards got shuffled and you had to start over.

Your friends had gone off to college, your friends were working on their own family, and the city evolved from when you last knew it.

You ate that last piece of chocolate so you could open a new box.

You come to a decision in the game of life of what to do next.

Do you want children?

Or would you rather go back to school?

Do you want a family?

And just as you decide how to play those cards, eat that piece of chocolate, or choose the next path in the game of life a tornado hit.

You were in a car accident with very little chance of survival. Your memory is gone for approximately 6 months.

All your Uno cards get reshuffled.

You hit a dead end in the game of life.

You can't find any more desirable chocolate in the house.

All of a sudden you are at a point where you need to relearn everything from walking to eating to taking care of yourself. And of course this got to be frustration when you just couldn't do it. It was something that you used to be able to do, so why can't you know? You had to figure out a new plan for the cards in your hand.

Your mind was filled with the idea of the left sided people. It was to fill a void in time that your brain had lost.

The left sided people could only use the left side. This is a true story for me, Subconsciously I used my fingers to show '3' which was in my mind the 3rd floor. My mind came up with this crazy idea that I was abducted when I was on a camping trip by aliens that could only use their left side. Talk about imaginary illusions and people.

I was hit on the left side of my brain and that controls the right side of my body. I wasn't able to use my right side as well as the left side and so I often resorted to using that left side. I perceived it as uninjured when in fact there really is no way to tell how injured you really are.

The best part is that I was right handed. I had two options; I could choose not to write or to learn to write with the left hand. My left hand writing skills are shaky but it is readable! I try to practice writing left handed to this day.

It was also difficult for you to swallow so you started on feeding tubes. Slowly you got the chance to eat in the dining room.

Except everything was pureed and you were under the rules of a bite of found followed by a drink. Since you had to have thickened liquids you got orange and occasionally cranberry at every meal.

Somehow that undesirable piece of chocolate became desirable again. The only way to reach further was to eat it and move on up.

All the choices in the game of life made sense now and allowed you to follow that path of your recovery.

The cards you played now make up your success or your failure at this point. You could play different cards to get back on track.

On track to a place where you should be, where you left when you had that car accident.

Or maybe getting back on track would screw you up again?

Perhaps you might have found that box of chocolate empty causing the need to go buy another box.

Or maybe you have a detour in the game of life such as a career change or additional children. These would all add to the day to day of your current life.

Before my accident I wanted to be a math teacher. I loved kids and was very good at math.

With the speech problem, I personally didn't think teaching would be a great idea and so I switched to accounting. I can imagine it now, trying to teach and have all your students look at you confused, What did she say?

So what if you could find some meaning in your recovery?

How did all the games of connect 4 and picking up sticks contribute to where you are now?

How did the constant swallowing exercises help you to where you are now?

How did the early art scene creations help you where you are now?

Why did you only get thickened orange juice?

Why couldn't you pick up that ham and cheese sandwich with your hands?

Why couldn't you leave this building unsupervised?

Why couldn't you have what you wanted then?

Why?

All of these things only pushed you to get stronger now so that you could have regular food.

So you could have that shake from McDonalds.

So you could have that coke that was all around you.

So you could just be you. Doing what you want when you want to.

So you could be a contributing part of society.

So now you could have a box of chocolates with only the ones you liked.

So, you were able to win the game of life with a career that you desired, with a passion that you lived, and surrounded by people that cared by you.

So, you could place that last card in Uno and declare victory

This is you now!

I took up cycling as a form of rehabilitation. Riding allowed me to feel free from everything around me.

I progressed through a few types of trikes before I was invited to a military paracycling camp.

They had handcycles and upright bikes. Since my balance is off due to being half deaf in my right ear I took a handcycle.

The first time I took it out went ok but then the next day I threw out my shoulder, enough of that.

The coach there told me about a trike and at first I was thinking hell no but he showed me a picture and it looked really cool! The coach hooked me up with a trike rider who is my coach today.

Even after recovery you may encounter a challenge that diverts you back to the game of life or even the box of chocolates.

The US classified me as a WT1 but I was mistakenly entered as a WT2 when I went to South Africa. The higher the class the less of an impact your disability has on you. Boy was I pissed. I dislike getting beaten by sometimes 10 minutes.

I placed last in South Africa and awards had started before I finished. Frustration begins to set in and I don't think those last few miles were performed at my greatest ability.

However it pushed me to train more and learn ways as a competitive advantage such as standing and pedaling.

As I continued to race I still placed last but the time gap started to get shorter. There seemed to be less frustration going on as well.

My ultimate goal is to race in the Paralympics and I hope to make it there one day. I keep in mind that I am still younger than many and as I improve, their performance may decline. That just makes competing more intense and awesome!

That job you earned before the accident may not all be that desirable any more. Frustration and confusion begin to set in.

What could I have done better?

Can I remedy this in any way?

Back to the game of life you go. You already have most of your education so you find a new career and get educated towards that.

Happiness comes when you find a new job that fits you well.

A black cheep is thrown into your path and messes with everything that you may have worked your recovery up to.

In my case the tax credit for hiring a disabled veteran was running out and the company was being sold. Nothing was going in my favor here and it was very frustrating. Not to mention annoying.

But I endured and so can you!

You are thrown backwards in the game of life.

You take a bite on a piece of undesirable chocolate.

You lay a card in UNO that will come back to haunt you.

You go back to a point where you must endure the suffering or accept it once again.

Just in the game of life you have a choice; either accept it or stand up for what is right.

The choice is ultimately yours but know that if you know you are right then why accept blame for something that you did not do?

That's where society is in part to blame. They perceive those who have a brain injury, who are disabled in some way as different than the general population.

In some ways they are accurate, you may look differently, you may talk differently, and you may act differently.

But what society does not realize is that some of these individuals do not take no for an answer.

This might not describe you currently, but it should.

I fought this as hard as I could and I'm sure that I lost a few good people but maybe they were in it from the start?

From the CPA who went on FMLA leave right before it started and came back within days of you leaving to finding changed performance documents.

Boy was that frustrating!

Find your way back into the game of life. Find a new path that will work with you.

Play a card in UNO that will work for you.

Gain something in the game of life that will help you.

Eat another piece of desirable chocolate.

You are unique and there is no one like you. You have a right to be equal!

And when someone plays an undesirable card in UNO, find a way to turn it in your favor.

Do you reverse and hope that they don't reverse again so that you can play an undesirable card next round?

Strategize your game of life in hopes that it will turn out best for you.

Finish up that box of undesirable chocolates and get to a better box if any at all. Find a flavor that you like.

And make that flavor now, what will guide your life and where you want to take it.

In that accident I got a severe TBI, brain stem damage, pulverized spleen, and my stomach was up in my chest. I had a broken collar bone as well.

As a result of the brain injury and brain stem injury I developed right ear hearing loss, a voice disorder known as dysarthria, double vision, and right side hemiparesis.

My cards were definitely shuffled and it seemed that there were no more desirable pieces of chocolate.

Doctors told my parents to put me in a nursing home and get on with their life. I was given a minimal chance of living.

But the cards were shuffled in both UNO and the game of life.

They played cards for me and I got a second chance at life.

How many people can honestly say that?

Can you?

People don't wake up from a coma overnight. Instead it is gradual. For me there is a void of approximately 6 months of memory that are missing. I go by what I am told happened and that will have to suffice for now.

During recovery the void in my brain were filled with made up stories such as the left sided people, where you were only able to use the left side of your body.

The cards were played well at the Rehabilitation Institute of Chicago until they could no longer be played.

The therapists thought that they could help me no more. Although it was both confusion and excitement at the time, I think they did it based on the current situation.

So they sent me home with a new set of cards. A new set that was used to adapt to my current situation.

I couldn't get better anymore, right?

Well doctors and the therapists were wrong, this was only the beginning.

There was signs of excitement in the air along with signs of both confusion and frustration.

With those cards I went from a wheelchair to a walker to a cane to sometimes walking with nothing.

I went back to school, earned the top grade in my calculus class. Getting around the college campus was very difficult. The elevators were on one side of the building while my classes were on the other side of the building and in between was a heavy glass door partition.

I earned my AS and BS in Accounting and went on to earn my MS in Forensic Accounting. I found a college where I could learn online. I taught myself how to do pretty much everything that we going to be tested on. And of course there were the daily google and youtube searches on how to do it.

My parents, sister, and my sister's husband traveled to Florida for my Bachelor's graduation.

2 years later we would travel to New Hampshire for my Master's.

(I was tired in this photo and just wanted to go to bed)

It was exciting to finish a program such as rigorous as this was and on my own! Not to mention a 3.93 GPA! How awesome is that?

I relearned how to drive. Getting back behind the wheel when I was nearly killed by one was very frightening especially for my mom. We found a car with side air bags and all the safety features. I used a spinning knob, a panoramic mirror, and a turn signal extender. I still use them to this day but I can't complain about that. Well except when I have to drive a rental car. That can cause trouble.

I relearned how to live on my own. My first time living on my own was in an apartment in an assisted living community. It was down the road from both my parents and my grandma. It was simply awesome and amazing!

I learned how to manage my finances and support myself. I kept a checkbook and made sure that I kept most of the money I needed to pay my bills.

I relearned how to cook. Sometimes I'd set off the fire alarm trying to cook but hey who doesn't?

I bought my own condo. About 3 years after moving into the apartment the income from my job made me ineligible to live there. I found a condo across the street and continue to call that home. Plus I could ride with crossing a busy street and did not have to rent a storage space.

My cards were all played well in the game of life.

No cards were played in UNO to stall me.

I had a fresh box of chocolate to go with.

But soon my game of life would need to turn sour.

An opponent would play a card in UNO that would haunt me.

Pieces of undesirable chocolates come before me and they would have to be eaten.

The game of life had taken a wrong turn.

There was still a negative stigma against disabled people.

Many just didn't think we were equal to abled bodied people.

We are treated differently.

We just have to laugh at this sometimes and try to keep our spirits high.

My voice doesn't match my mind and that confuses the heck out of people sometimes. They can't grasp the fact that I have a Master's degree and in Forensic Accounting!

I can't tell you how many times I have had employers hang up on me. They usually hang up on me the moment I start to speak.

One of the tools I learned early in my job search was to write everything down as soon as possible after. That way you have proof in the event that you need it.

In one case I had my mom call back and they tried to tell her it was for a customer service position that involved the phone although they told me it was for an accounting clerk position when they first called.

Its very frustrating and often very offensive that they can do that and get away with it. But it's often their word against yours.

And guess what? They usually win because of the supposed strength of their mind and ability.

I was upset but I got over it. Getting over it may take more time than others and those around you simply do not understand why. No two injuries are alike. Especially brain injuries since no two people are raised the exact same way or are injured in the exact same manner.

Or the many times I got called sweetie when I was with my mom. I really do wish people would pay attention to how they treat others.

Is that how you want to be treated? What if I came back and called you that?

The game of UNO, the game of Life, and as well as the box of chocolates keep playing out in my life.

As I am writing this, my accident was over 12 years ago and I still feel the negativity and discrimination in the air.

I have heard others talk about me behind my back. Even though I have lost some of my hearing, my other ear hears twice as much. I can also lip read.

I have heard others try to talk about me in Spanish. I took Spanish in high school but they usually don't know that. I just let them talk and go about my business.

I really can't change their thoughts or can I?

Can you change others beliefs and perceptions?

I have had people try to tell me what to do because they think they know better than me. I wish they could just see how they are treating me.

I have been accused of other's mistakes just because I had one problem.

As these examples happen I am thrown back in the game of life, have to play an undesirable card in UNO, or eat an undesirable piece of chocolate.

And the cycle continues.

I was discharged from a job that I did well. The circumstances and information around it are very iffy. From what I can tell the tax credit for hiring a disabled veteran was expiring.

Or the company that bought them out didn't have a need for my position anymore.

Does it matter that I caught an order that was over a million dollars only to find out that it was entered incorrectly?

Does it matter that could have cost the company I worked for a lot in legal fees or even the company that ordered it a lot of money?

The person in charge of letting me go clearly wasn't thinking!

But instead he took the easy way out by changing a positive review to look negative in an effort to make it look like I was having a problem since day 1.

I was mad and upset and probably pissed off a lot of people in the following months but what can you expect?

Would you act the same way if you were treated wrongly?

How would you go about changing it?

It seemed that I was thrown back in the game of life and there seemed to be no way going forward.

Throughout this I continued to Para cycle. I made gains in my performance but there was still a major difference in the ability levels.

My dream to compete in the Paralympics seemed to be slipping away and there was nothing that I could do about it. Or was there?

I had eaten an undesirable piece of chocolate.

My gaming partner played a pick two in Uno.

I encountered a debt in the game of life.

Weeks later I went to a ride that I have done before. I didn't have a riding partner and so I was going to ride alone.

But they found out and wouldn't let that happen!

They paired me up with a group and I had a blast.

When we got back I even got to try riding stoker in the tandem. That was awesome and I want to hopefully develop that.

And so I thought that I was going to win this game of life;

Finish off the box of chocolates with a desirable piece of chocolate;

And play my last card in UNO.

Well that didn't happen and I got thrown back in the game of life.

I got in trouble again for something that wasn't my fault. Talk about frustration!

This is never ending,

There really is a negative stigma against disabled people and often those people are unaware of their actions.

Sometimes it just seems like you can't get ahead but trust me there is a way!

It's called "you"!

Only you can decide what you are doing and no one can take that away from you.

People may keep trying,

But hey it's life!

Are you ready for it?

Embrace the challenges!

Are you doing what you are called to do?

Each day there is some new challenge that I must face.

Many of the places I frequently visit have people that know me and can help me if needed.

There will always be challenges to face when others don't seem to understand why you can't use a phone.

Can't you use a TTY? If only my typing was fast enough for that and it would definitely make things easier!

People can't seem to understand why I get upset over little things. I have no filter, remember the car accident?

Even though I have a memory that can remember the finer details of something, I am often ignored as a witness.

With each challenge I aim to push forward.

To be the best version of myself.

So I can climb mountains.

So I can swing along the trees in south Africa.

Each of the trials that I have faced can only help me get further in life.

I didn't survive that accident to have no purpose in life.

I am a fighter and working on getting people to realize that we are equal.

Don't you feel the same way?

How is life treating you now?

Do you know your purpose in life?

Made in the USA
Monee, IL
29 September 2022

14905090R00016